Dear Parents and Educators,

Welcome to Penguin Young Readers! As parents and educators, you know that each child develops at his or her own pace—in terms of speech, critical thinking, and, of course, reading. Penguin Young Readers recognizes this fact. As a result, each Penguin Young Readers book is assigned a traditional easy-to-read level (1–4) as well as a Guided Reading Level (A–P). Both of these systems will help you choose the right book for your child. Please refer to the back of each book for specific leveling information. Penguin Young Readers features esteemed authors and illustrators, stories about favorite characters, fascinating nonfiction, and more!

Young Cam Jansen and the Dinosaur Game

LEVEL **3**

GUIDED READING LEVEL **J**

This book is perfect for a **Transitional Reader** who:
• can read multisyllable and compound words;
• can read words with prefixes and suffixes;
• is able to identify story elements (beginning, middle, end, plot, setting, characters, problem, solution); and
• can understand different points of view.

Here are some **activities** you can do during and after reading this book:
• Problem/Solution: Throughout the story, there are many problems. But for each problem, there is a solution. For example, when Cam's dad can't find the party invitation (problem), Cam uses her photographic memory to remember the address and time of the party (solution). Look through the book for other problems and their solutions.
• Character Traits: Cam is a very interesting character. Come up with a list of words to describe her.

Remember, sharing the love of reading with a child is the best gift you can give!

—Bonnie Bader, EdM, and Katie Carella, EdM
    Penguin Young Readers program

*Penguin Young Readers are leveled by independent reviewers applying the standards developed by Irene Fountas and Gay Su Pinnell in *Matching Books to Readers: Using Leveled Books in Guided Reading*, Heinemann, 1999.

Penguin Young Readers
Published by the Penguin Group
Penguin Group (USA) Inc., 375 Hudson Street, New York, New York 10014, USA
Penguin Group (Canada), 90 Eglinton Avenue East, Suite 700, Toronto,
Ontario M4P 2Y3, Canada
(a division of Pearson Penguin Canada Inc.)
Penguin Books Ltd., 80 Strand, London WC2R 0RL, England
Penguin Group Ireland, 25 St. Stephen's Green, Dublin 2, Ireland (a division of Penguin Books Ltd.)
Penguin Group (Australia), 250 Camberwell Road, Camberwell, Victoria 3124, Australia
(a division of Pearson Australia Group Pty. Ltd.)
Penguin Books India Pvt. Ltd., 11 Community Centre, Panchsheel Park, New Delhi—110 017, India
Penguin Group (NZ), 67 Apollo Drive, Rosedale, Auckland 0632, New Zealand
(a division of Pearson New Zealand Ltd.)
Penguin Books (South Africa) (Pty.) Ltd., 24 Sturdee Avenue, Rosebank,
Johannesburg 2196, South Africa

Penguin Books Ltd., Registered Offices: 80 Strand, London WC2R 0RL, England

The Library of Congress has cataloged the Viking edition under
the following Control Number: 95046463

ISBN 978-0-14-037779-8   10 9 8

Young Cam Jansen
and the Dinosaur Game

by David A. Adler
illustrated by Susanna Natti

Penguin Young Readers
An Imprint of Penguin Group (USA) Inc.

Contents

Chapter 1
I'm Going! I'm Going!

Honk! Honk!

"I'm going! I'm going!"

Mr. Jansen said.

He was driving his daughter Cam

and her friend Eric Shelton

to a birthday party.

Mr. Jansen stopped at the corner.

He looked at the street signs.

Then he said, "I'm sorry.

I forgot where the party is.

And I forgot to bring the invitation."

Honk! Honk!

"I'm going! I'm going!"

Mr. Jansen said as he drove on.

"But I don't know *where* I'm going."

Mr. Jansen drove to the next corner
and parked the car.

Eric said, "I'm sure Cam remembers
where the party is."

Cam closed her eyes and said, "Click!"
Cam always closes her eyes
and says, "Click!" when she wants
to remember something.

Cam has an amazing memory.

"My memory is like a camera,"

she says.

"I have a picture in my head

of everything I've seen.

Click! is the sound my camera makes."

Cam's real name is Jennifer.

But because of her great memory,

people started to call her

"the Camera."

Then "the Camera" became

just "Cam."

"I'm looking at the invitation,"

Cam said, with her eyes closed.

"It says, 'Come to a party for Jane Bell.

3:00 p.m., 86 Robin Lane.'"

Cam opened her eyes.

Mr. Jansen drove to 86 Robin Lane.

There were balloons

and a big HAPPY BIRTHDAY sign

on the front door.

Mr. Bell opened the door and said,

"Come in. Come in."

He pointed to a big jar.

"Before you join the others,

guess how many dinosaurs are

in this jar.

Remember your guess.

The best one wins the dinosaurs."

The jar was filled with

blue, green, yellow, and red

toy dinosaurs.

Next to the jar were slips of paper,

a pen, and a shoe box.

Cam tried to count the dinosaurs.

But she couldn't.

Lots of dinosaurs were hidden

behind other dinosaurs.

Cam wrote her guess

on a slip of paper.

She put the paper in the shoe box.

Eric looked at the jar.

He looked for a long time.

Then he wrote his guess
on a slip of paper, too.
He put the paper in the shoe box.
Eric said, "I hope I win."
Then Cam and Eric went to
the kitchen.
Their friends were there,
sitting around the table.

Chapter 2
The Dinosaur Game

Mrs. Bell said, "Good, everyone is here.

I'll get the birthday cake."

She carried a large cake to the table.

Mrs. Bell lit the candles.

Everyone sang "Happy Birthday."

Then Mrs. Bell gave each child

a piece of birthday cake.

They were all eating cake

when Mr. Bell walked into the room.

13

"I counted the dinosaurs," he said.

"There were 154 in the jar."

Eric said, "I guessed 150.

Maybe I'll win."

Rachel said, "I guessed 300."

"Who won?" Jane asked.

"Who won the dinosaur game?"

Mr. Bell smiled.

"We'll see," he said,

"as soon as I have some cake."

When Mr. Bell finished,

he brought in the shoe box.

He turned it over and picked up

a slip of paper.

"180," he read.

Then he showed it to everyone.

"That was my guess," Jane said.

One by one Mr. Bell read the guesses.
"100 . . . 300 . . . 1,000 . . . 450 . . . 200."

Cam said, "200 was my guess."

Mr. Bell looked at the next slip of paper.

He read, "150."

"That was my guess," Eric said.

Then Mr. Bell held up the last slip of
paper and read, "154."

"That's mine," Robert said.

"I win."

"You *do* win," Mr. Bell said.

"You guessed the exact number.

And here's your prize."

He gave Robert the jar of dinosaurs.

Cam looked at Robert.

Then she looked at the slip of paper

in Mr. Bell's hand and said, "Click!"

Eric whispered to Cam,

"That's amazing.

He guessed the exact number

of dinosaurs."

"Yes," Cam said.

"It is amazing.

It's almost *too* amazing."

Chapter 3
Click!

Robert spilled the dinosaurs

onto the table.

"They're cute," Rachel said.

"Can I have one?" Jason asked.

Rachel asked, "Can I have one, too?"

"I'm not giving them away," Robert said.

"I'm selling them."

"I want a red one," Rachel said.

"I'll give you the money
at school tomorrow."
"I want three green dinosaurs
and two yellows," Jason said.

Mr. Bell said,

"Now let's play musical chairs."

He set six chairs in a line.

He turned on some music.

Then Mr. Bell told the children,

"Walk around the chairs.

When the music stops, sit down.

Whoever can't find a seat

is out of the game."

The children walked
around the chairs.
But not Cam.
She looked at the chairs.
She counted them.
Then she closed her eyes
and said, "Click!"

Chapter 4
You Made Me Lose

The music stopped.

Everyone but Cam sat down.

She was out of the game.

Mr. Bell took one chair away and

turned on the music again.

Cam opened her eyes.

She went over to the table.

She looked at the

slips of paper.

Then, as Eric walked past,

she whispered to him,

"I have something to show you."

Eric turned, and the music stopped.

Everyone but Eric sat down.

He was out of the game.

Mr. Bell took one chair away

and turned on the music again.

When Robert walked past,

Cam whispered to him,

"And I have something to show you."

Robert turned, and the music stopped.

Everyone but Robert sat down.

Robert was out of the game.

He told Cam, "You made me lose

at musical chairs."

Cam said, "And I'll make you lose

the dinosaurs, too."

Chapter 5
I'm Sharing

Cam said to Robert, "You wrote 154
after Jane's father counted
the dinosaurs."

"I did not!" Robert said.

Cam told him, "Mr. Bell turned over
the shoe box.

The papers fell out upside down.

They fell out in the same order
they were put in.

Jane's guess was first.

Eric and I were the last
to come to the party.
Our guesses should have been last.
But yours was."
Robert said, "Maybe the papers
got mixed up."
Cam told him, "There were eight guesses
but only seven kids are at the party.
You guessed twice.
You guessed when you came to the party.
You guessed again after
Jane's father told us there were
154 dinosaurs in the jar."
"I did not," Robert said.

Cam picked up Robert's winning guess.
"And look at this," she said.
Cam pointed to a chocolate smudge.
"You wrote this after we had
birthday cake.
That's why there's chocolate on it."

Cam and Eric looked at Robert's hands.
There was chocolate on them, too.
Robert looked down.

"You're right," he said softly.

"My real guess was 1,000 dinosaurs."

Robert put the dinosaurs back in the jar.

After the game of musical chairs ended,

Robert talked to Mrs. Bell.

He told her that Eric had really won

the dinosaur game.

Mrs. Bell gave the jar to Eric.

Rachel said, "I want to buy

a red dinosaur."

Jason said, "I want three green
dinosaurs and two yellows."
Eric told them, "I'm not selling
the dinosaurs.
I'm sharing them."
The children sat in a circle.
Eric walked around them.
"One for you," he said
as he gave each child a dinosaur.

"And one for you.

And one for you."

After Eric had given everyone else

a dinosaur he put one on an empty

chair and said, "And one for me."

Eric walked around the circle

again and again.

He walked around until

the big jar of toy dinosaurs was empty.

A Cam Jansen Memory Game

Take another look at the picture on page 6.
Study it.
Blink your eyes and say, "Click!"
Then turn back to this page
and answer these questions:

1. Are Cam's eyes open or closed?

2. What color are the stripes on Eric's shirt?

3. Is Mr. Jansen wearing a seat belt?

4. What color is Mr. Jansen's car?

5. What color is the ribbon in Cam's hair?

6. Does Mr. Jansen have both his hands on the car's steering wheel?